MICHAEL?
DID YOU THROW UP IN THERE?
NO, JUST POOPIN' YOU KNOW HOW I BE

WELL, I AM TAKING RESPONSIBILITY
IT IS UP TO ME TO GET RID OF THE CURSE THAT HIT MEREDITH WITH MY CAR
I'M NOT SUPERSTITIOUS
BUT... I'M... I AM A LITTLE-STITIOUS

TOBY IS IN HR, WHICH TECHNICALLY MEANS HE WORKS FOR CORPORATE
SO HE'S REALLY NOT A PART OF OUR FAMILY
ALSO, HE'S DIVORCED
SO HE'S REALLY NOT A PART OF HIS FAMILY

IF THE DEVIL WERE TO EXPLODE
AND EVIL WERE GONE FOREVER
WHAT SORT OF PARTY WOULD YOU HAVE?
LIKE A BEACH BLOWOUT?

WELL, THERE'S SOMEBODY I'D LIKE YOU TO MEET. SOMEBODY ELSE WHO HAS BEEN TO PRISON, WHO CAN TELL YOU WHAT IT IS REALLY LIKE
I'M PRISON MIKE. YOU KNOW WHY THEY CALL ME PRISON MIKE?
DO YOU REALLY EXPECT US TO BELIEVE YOU'RE SOMEBODY ELSE?
DO YOU REALLY EXPECT ME NOT TO PUSH YOU UP AGAINST THE WALL, BIOCH?

I LEARNED A WHILE BACK THAT IF I DON'T TEXT 911
PEOPLE WILL NOT RETURN MY CALLS
UM, BUT NOW PEOPLE ALWAYS RETURN MY CALLS
BECAUSE THEY THINK THAT SOMETHING HORRIBLE HAS HAPPENED

IN AN OFFICE, WHEN YOU ARE RANKING PEOPLE
CAPTAIN
MANAGER IS HIGHER THAN CAPTAIN
CAPTAIN
ON A BOAT, WHO KNOWS?
CAPTAIN
IT'S NEBULOSE
CAPTAIN

CHILDREN CANNOT LIE
THEY ARE INNOCENT AND THEY SPEAK THE TRUTH
AND OUT OF THE MOUTHS OF BABES
MICHAEL SCOTT IS FREAKING COOL

HOW COME CHRIS ROCK CAN DO A ROUTINE AND EVERYBODY FINDS IT HILARIOUS
AND GROUND-BREAKING AND THEN I GO AND DO THE EXACT SAME ROUTINE, SAME COMEDIC TIMING
AND PEOPLE FILE A COMPLAINT TO CORPORATE?
IS IT BECAUSE I'M WHITE AND CHRIS IS BLACK?

YOU MAY LOOK AROUND
AND SEE TWO GROUPS HERE
WHITE COLLAR, BLUE COLLAR
BUT I DON'T SEE IT THAT WAY
AND YOU KNOW WHY NOT?
BECAUSE I AM
COLLAR-BLIND

YOU'RE KIDDING ME! GOD! YOU SAY RADON IS SILENT BUT DEADLY AND THEN YOU EXPECT ME NOT TO MAKE FARTING NOISES WITH MY MOUTH?
WHAT IS THIS?!
YOU KNOW WHAT WE'RE NOT GOING TO DIE OF RADON
WE'RE GOING TO DIE OF BOREDOM

SO RYAN GOT PROMOTED TO CORPORATE, WHERE HE IS A LITTLE FISH IN A BIG POND
WHEREAS BACK HERE IN SCRANTON I AM STILL TOP DOG IN A FAIRLY LARGE POND
SO WHO IS THE REAL BOSS?
THE DOG OR A FISH?

DO I NEED TO BE LIKED? ABSOLUTELY NOT
I LIKE TO BE LIKED I ENJOY BEING LIKED I HAVE TO BE LIKED
BUT IT'S NOT LIKE A COMPULSIVE NEED TO BE LIKED
LIKE MY NEED TO BE PRAISED

LISTEN, I LIKE KIDS

BUT THIS IS NOT
A KID'S ENVIRONMENT

THIS IS LIKE HBO,
NO LIMITS

WHO KNOWS WHAT
I'M GOING TO SAY?

CRAZY STUFF

AND IT IS R RATED,
IT IS NOT RATED G

I AM LIKE
EDDIE MURPHY IN RAW

AND THEY ARE TRYING TO
MAKE ME INTO EDDIE MURPHY
IN DADDY DAYCARE

BOTH GREAT MOVIES
BUT, STILL

WEBSTER'S DICTIONARY DEFINES 'WEDDING' AS THE FUSING OF TWO METALS WITH A HOT TORCH
WELL YOU KNOW SOMETHING
I THINK YOU GUYS ARE TWO MEDALS
GOLD MEDALS

I JUST DON'T WANT YOU TO LIE TO ME. I DON'T WANT YOU TO EVER LIE TO ME
HAVE I EVER LIED TO YOU?
YEAH
I JUST DON'T WANT YOU TO

IF I HAD A GUN
WITH TWO BULLETS
AND I WAS IN A ROOM WITH HITLER, BIN LADEN AND TOBY
I WOULD SHOOT TOBY TWICE

AND I KNEW EXACTLY
WHAT TO DO
BUT IN A MUCH MORE REAL SENSE
I HAD NO IDEA WHAT TO DO

GUESS WHAT
I HAVE FLAWS
WHAT ARE THEY?
OH I DUNNO
I SING IN THE SHOWER
SOMETIMES I SPEND TOO MUCH TIME VOLUNTEERING
OCCASIONALLY I'LL HIT SOMEBODY WITH MY CAR
SO SUE ME... NO, DON'T SUE ME
THAT IS OPPOSITE THE POINT I'M TRYING TO MAKE

I'M AN EARLY BIRD
AND I'M A NIGHT OWL
SO I'M WISE
AND I HAVE WORMS

SOMETIMES I'LL START A SENTENCE, AND I DON'T EVEN KNOW WHERE IT'S GOING
I JUST HOPE I FIND IT ALONG THE WAY
LIKE AN IMPROV CONVERSATION
AN IMPROVERSATION

YEAH, I WENT HUNTING ONCE
SHOT THE DEER IN THE LEG
HAD TO KILL IT WITH A SHOVEL
TOOK ABOUT AN HOUR. WHY DO YOU ASK?

JAN IS COLD

IF SHE WAS SITTING ACROSS FROM YOU ON A TRAIN

AND SHE WASN'T MOVING

YOU MIGHT THINK SHE WAS DEAD

IS THERE A GOD?
IF NOT
WHAT ARE ALL THE CHURCHES FOR?
AND WHO IS JESUS' DAD?

IF THIS WAS RUSSIA THEN YEAH, SURE
EVERYONE WOULD GO TO ONE SANTA
AND THERE WOULD BE A LINE AROUND THE BLOCK
AND ONCE YOU SAT ON HER LAP
AND SHE ASKED YOU WHAT YOU WANTED
YOU WOULD PROBABLY SAY FREEDOM
AT WHICH POINT THE KGB WOULD ARREST YOU
AND SEND YOU TO SERBIA
IT'S A GOOD THING RUSSIA DOESN'T EXIST ANYMORE

WHEN I SAID THAT I WAS KING OF FORWARDS

YOU GOT TO UNDERSTAND THAT I DON'T COME UP WITH THIS STUFF

I JUST FORWARD IT ALONG

YOU WOULDN'T ARREST A GUY WHO WAS JUST PASSING DRUGS FROM ONE GUY TO ANOTHER

YES, IT IS TRUE
I, MICHAEL SCOTT
AM SIGNING UP WITH AN ONLINE DATING SERVICE
THOUSANDS OF PEOPLE HAVE DONE IT
AND I AM GOING TO DO IT
I NEED A USERNAME
AND I HAVE A GREAT ONE
LITTLE KID LOVER
THAT WAY PEOPLE WILL KNOW EXACTLY WHERE MY PRIORITIES ARE AT

I'M MC MIKE SCOTT, AND I AM HOT

SHE'S DJ JAZZY FLAX
AND SHE IS THE BEST

ALL THOSE SUCKER BRANCHES
CAN SUCK OUR FAT

WIKKA WIKKA WIKKA WHAT

DAVID HERE IT IS. MY PHILOSOPHY IS BASICALLY THIS.
AND THIS IS SOMETHING THAT I LIVE BY
AND I ALWAYS HAVE AND I ALWAYS WILL
DON'T, EVER, FOR ANY REASON, DO ANYTHING, TO ANYONE, FOR ANY REASON, EVER
NO MATTER WHAT, NO MATTER WHERE, OR WHO OR WHO YOU ARE WITH
OR OR WHERE YOU ARE GOING
OR, OR WHERE YOU'VE BEEN, EVER
FOR ANY REASON
WHATSOEVER

THAT IS A PERFECTLY GOOD MINI CHRISTMAS TREE
WE ARE GOING TO SELL THAT TO CHARITY
BECAUSE THAT IS WHAT CHRISTMAS IS ALL ABOUT

GREAT PRACTICAL JOKE JIM
YOU GOT ME TO GO TO THE ANNEX
HI, MICHA-
NOOOO! GOD!
NO, GOD, PLEASE NO!
NO! NO!
NOOO!

WOMEN CAN'T HAVE FUN

IF THEY DON'T FEEL SAFE

FOR EXAMPLE

JAN AND I HAVE
A SAFE WORD IN CASE
THINGS GO TOO FAR

FOLIAGE

AND IF ONE OF US
SAYS THAT WORD

THE OTHER ONE
HAS TO STOP

ALTHOUGH LAST TIME...

SHE PRETENDED
SHE DIDN'T HEAR ME

UM, PAM, I HAVE TO LET SOMEBODY GO TODAY
THIS IS, UH, THE HARDEST THING I'VE EVER HAD TO DO
WHY DID YOU PUT IT OFF UNTIL HALLOWEEN?
BECAUSE IT'S VERY SCARY STUFF

YOU KNOW WHAT THEY SAY
FOOL ME ONCE, STRIKE ONE
BUT FOOL ME TWICE...
STRIKE THREE

YEAH
I'M TRYING TO LURE THESE KIDS INTO MY BOOTH
BUT UH, KIDS ARE VERY WARY ABOUT BEING "LURED" THESE DAYS
THANK YOU DATELINE!

HO HO HO!
WHY PAY MORE TO SIT NEXT TO
OLD TRANNY CLAUS OVER THERE
WHEN YOU CAN SIT ON MY LAP
PHYLLIS IS ONLY
PRETENDING TO BE A MAN
I'M THE REAL THING
SIT DOWN ON MY LAP
AND THERE WILL BE NO DOUBT

TWO QUEENS ON CASINO NIGHT
I AM GOING TO DROP A DEUCE ON EVERYBODY

I'VE ALWAYS WANTED TO BE IN THE WITNESS PROTECTION PROGRAM
FRESH START NO DEBTS NO BAGGAGE
I'VE ALREADY GOT MY NAME PICKED OUT, LORD RUPERT EVERTON
I'M A SHIPPING MERCHANT WHO RAISES FANCY DOGS THAT'S THE LIFE

WHEN THE SON OF THE DEPOSED KING OF NIGERIA EMAILS YOU DIRECTLY ASKING FOR HELP
YOU HELP!
HIS FATHER RAN THE FREAKING COUNTRY!
OK!?

YOU WANNA HEAR A LIE?
WHAT?
I... THINK YOU'RE GREAT
YOU'RE MY BEST FRIEND

Made in the USA
Monee, IL
13 December 2019

18540326R00046